CAN I PUT IT A VOLCANO?

Ben Wilmshurst

"Woah, woah, woah,
don't do that!"
Who on earth are you?
        "I'm Dr. Taylor."
Ooh, can you take a
quick look at this rash...
"I'm not that kind of doctor,
I'm a volcanologist."

Like this?

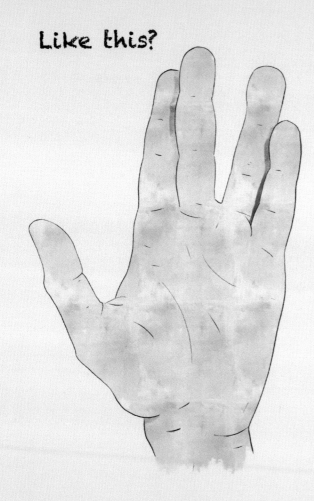

"No, no, are you trying to get sued? It's volcanoes, not Vulcans."
So, what, you give volcanoes CPR?

"No..."
Wait, I've got a better one... you give them something for... heartburn...
...
Reflux?
...
If you had a son would you name him Ash?
...

There you go,
that's more
like it!

"All those years
studying for my PhD
and this is how I get
treated."

You can't just turn
away, it doesn't
work like that.

Well, these radioactive barrels aren't going to throw themselves into that grumpy hill.

"No, don't do that! Where did you even get that?"

I know a guy... he lives in a lair beneath the volcano.

"Well you can't just chuck it into the volcano, that won't get rid of it. In fact, a volcano is probably the last place you want to be dumping spent uranium. Do you want radioactive lava? Because that's how you get radioactive lava."

Oh... alright then... what about this truck full of regular ol'non-nuclear rubbish? Just a load of harmless ol' plastic and whatnot. Poppy in the volcano?

"No! What's wrong with you? You'll choke us all in toxic fumes and contaminate the ground."

Oh...

"And you'll likely rupture the surface of the lava and set off a wild set of explosive chain reactions that..."

Ok, ok, ok, what about if I plopped a big ice cube in there?

Would that help?

"Hey?"

"No, it doesn't work like that."

What if it was a really really

big

ice cube?

...

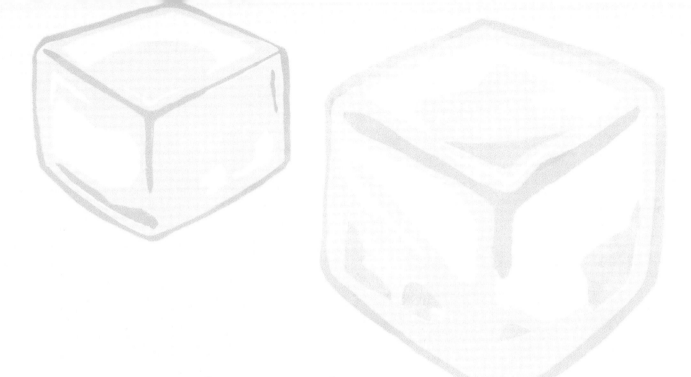

2 really really big ice cubes?
                "What would you be trying to achieve?"
I dunno... science?
                        "That's not... that's not science..."
You're not science.

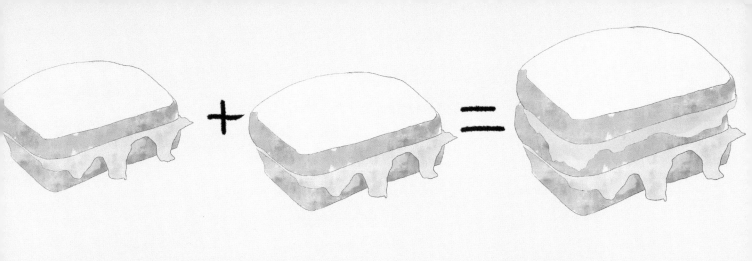

I think it'd be like making a double decker
cheese toastie.
"How can you possibly equate a volcano to a
cheese toastie?"
Well they're both hot... and they've got crusts...
and sit on plates...

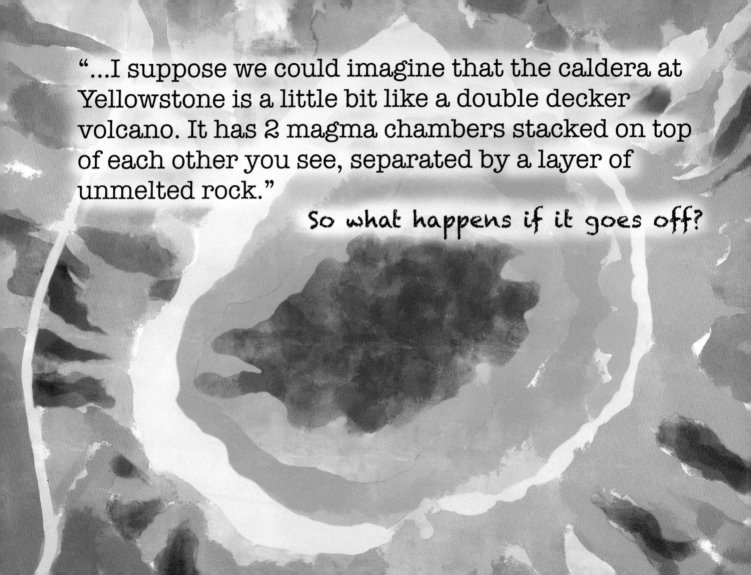

"...I suppose we could imagine that the caldera at Yellowstone is a little bit like a double decker volcano. It has 2 magma chambers stacked on top of each other you see, separated by a layer of unmelted rock."

So what happens if it goes off?

"Goes off? Goes off???
Milk goes off! Volcanoes
erupt! And in the case of
Yellowstone, we could be
in serious trouble."

How serious?

"Well we can't say for sure because there are so
many variables and so many unknowns, but we're
talking severe social and planetary effects... lava
flows, ash clouds..."

Yeh, it's happened again... please send help.

Well not literally...

"We'd have to consult someone with expertise... maybe someone at NASA."

What about the one ring to rule them all. One ring to find them, one ring to bring them all, and in the darkness bind them?

"WHAT DID I SAY ABOUT GETTING SUED!?"

How about that herd of sheep?
"I think you need a therapist."

Ok fine, how about INTOLERANCE

"Hey, look over there!"

Dr Taylor?

Dr. Taylor?

Printed in Great Britain
by Amazon